Murder Divided by 3

Three detectives originally from Florida meet in David, Panamá. Clint Faraday is retired from the US and is living on the Comarca Ngobe Bugle with his wife and son and daughter.

CD Grimes is a billionaire private detective from Bonita Springs, Florida. He is with his wife and flew in his own jet to David at the invitation of his nutty musician, botanist, author friend, Dave, who works with Clint Faraday quite often and is also a close friend of the Indios.

Nick Storie is there with his wife just to see the country. He has a place on Martinique. He is a police homicide detective with Naples South Station.

(Theses are the three detective series I wrote and am writing)

Dave finds a murder case for them. They can try to solve it, each with his own method.

It seems to be an ordinary sort of thing.

At first.

Contents

About the author

CD Moulton has traveled extensively over much of the world both in the music business, where he was a rock guitarist, songwriter and arranger and in an import/export business. He has been everything from a bar owner to auto salvage (junkyard) manager, longshoreman to high steel worker, orchid grower to landscaper, tropical fish farmer to commercial fisherman. He started writing books in 1983 and has published more than 350 books as of January 1, 2023. His most popular books to date are about research with orchids, though much of his science fiction and fantasy work has proven popular. He wrote the CD Grimes, PI series, and the Det. Nick Storie series, Clint Faraday series, and many other works.

He now resides in Gualaca, Chiriqui, Panamá, where he writes books, plays music with friends, does research with orchids and medicinal plants. He has lately become involved in fighting for the rights of the indigenous people, who are among his closest friends, and in fighting the extreme corruption in the courts and police in Panamá.

He offers the free e-book, *Fading Paradise*, that explains what he has been through because of the corruption.

CD is the discoverer of the Chadam Protocol for curing cancer.

Facebook page Ambrosia peruviana for cancer.

Clint Faraday, retired private detective from Florida, now residing on the Comarca Ngobe Bugle in Panamá, stretched and yawned. He went out on his porch overlooking the Caribbean in Cusapín with his first cup of coffee for the day. He was as much as addicted to the rich fine Panamanian coffee. It was really fresh, having been ground from the dried coffee beans his wife had brought from their place in the mountains near Quebrada Tula just yesterday afternoon.

It would be a good day. Beautiful sunrise.

Nito, his son, came with his daughter, Nicole, to hug him and head for the school in Cusapín. Clint and two friends had built several schools on the comarca, as well as hospitals and clinics.

His beautiful young (Clint was 69. Tyna was 28.) wife came to tease and play. She was going into Cusapín to help clean and sort the yuca, yampi, otoe and other root crop vegetables for storage and to take into Chiriqui Grande for the market.

"What are you doing today, Hon?" she asked, then thought. "Oh, yeah. Dave wants you to go to David to meet a friend from Florida he thinks you might know from being a detective there."

"I can handle the foundation and that kind of crap while I'm there. I'm getting a mite too old and cranky to have to go to David every time somebody sneezes.

"Dave wanted you to come."

"No. I'm sick of cities. I like it here."

"He said that he wanted to see the two most beautiful women in the world there together to watch the riots it would cause. Selma is going to be there. She knows the detective and his wife."

Selma Wentworth was Dave's ladyfriend. They had known each other in Florida before Dave moved to Panamá. She came to visit several years ago and, like Dave, never looked back at the states.

Like Clint, for that matter!

"You can run to Soloy while you're there. I think the museum branch there is about the most popular place near David. The government is still trying every trick it can think of to get it moved to Panamá City."

A case Clint had led to the discovery of a preserved pirate ship that had what turned out to be eleven billion dollars worth of gold and jewels. Clint had arranged to have the entire find registered as property of the Ngobes, which was merely the law in the constitution. He got the official declaration before the government knew what it was worth. He had found pirate treasure before that was sent to Panamá City – where more than eighty five percent of it disappeared.

"Not going to happen. All the publicity from all over the world guarantees they can only go so far."

"Well, I guess you won't be here for a few days, so I can move my fantastic lover in while you're gone. The trouble with that is I can't find anyone who can even offer you a little competition!"

They teased a few minutes longer, then Tyna headed for the town a little more than a kilometer away along the beach. Clint packed enough for four days and got in his boat to head for Chiriqui Grande, from where he drove his own car to David.

The trip was beautiful, across the mountains and the dam. He stopped in Hornitos and Gualaca to visit with friends for a few minutes. He arrived in David and checked into the Pensión Costa Rica and went to the restaurant across the street in the panaderia, then called Dave, who said he was just heading for the airport to meet CD.

Clint said he brought the car, so he could take him and bring his friends into David. It would save them taxi fare, at least.

"He flies his own twelve seater Lear jet? He's worried about a three dollar taxi bill?"

The only detective Clint ever heard of in Florida who could own a two million dollar jet that he flew himself was CD Grimes. He'd met him in Sarasota on a case some years ago. It involved massive theft from NASA. He knew what Dave meant about the two most beautiful women in the world. Alma Grimes was a total knockout.

"He'll want to go to the Hotel Ciudad David, I suppose."

"No. They'll stay at my place. They aren't anything like you'd expect. CD talks like he's a pompous ass, but it's his method. They're very real, very basic people."

"Well, I think we'll have a lot to talk about if he talks about his cases."

"Not too much. He likes fishing and seeing the country. He grows orchids, which is where I originally met him. Alma is as much into them. They'll be in heaven here!

"I send him a lot of the new things I find. We've already agreed to spend most of his time here all over the country."

"Hell, Dave! You've been here ten years and haven't seen half of it yourself! How long are they staying?"

"The nice thing about being a billionaire is that you stay as long as you damned well please!"

"It should prove interesting, at the very least!"

"Are you about ready?" Alma Grimes, wife of the semi-famous CD Grimes, billionaire private detective, called from the house. CD was in the cool house, a special greenhouse he had built underground so temperature and humidity could be controlled exactly.

"Just checking the autos," he replied. "Just think, love! We're going to the places Dave gathered a hundred or more of these plants. If Panamá is half of what the pictures tell, it's going to be a great vacation!"

"They're actual pictures. Dave doesn't change anything, so it will be just like that. I want to see the places he uses on the covers of his books."

"I think we'll really like Panamá. If that place on Isla San Cristobál, his Indio friend's finca, is still available, I'll probably buy it."

"Well, we can certainly make an orchid garden there with native species! There are more than twelve hundred listed species and Dave has listed probably ten dozen more. Most of the places he'll show us were never explored before he did it."

"He'll show us a lot of places that haven't been explored, so we can find a few new things for ourselves, knowing him. I can name one after you and you can name one after me!"

They joked a bit, ate a breakfast that was made from local seafoods they'd caught themselves, then got in the old Jeep CD liked and headed for the private airport in Englewood. Mike and Shirley talked awhile and they promised to say hello to Dave for them and to have them go to Panamá if it was half of what they expected. Tony Jacobi, CD's manager for "The Crane Crap" – a bunch of companies CD owned, and husband of Shirley, came to see that things would run smoothly while they were gone.

"Hell, Tony. You run them anyhow. Get JK to take care of anything we normal people can't handle!"

JK was John Kiley. He was an absolute genius with computers. CD had never found a problem he couldn't fix.

After half an hour or so they got in the jet and headed for Panamá.

The flight over the gulf and Caribbean was smooth. CD took a detour to fly over Kylvania, a group of islands southeast of Panamá that he had bought in a case and had given to JK. It was registered as an independent nation. He also flew over St. Wartons Island on the way, where he owned some property, as did Dave.

He landed at David and went through customs.

He expected more trouble than he got. Dave was there with a person he wanted CD and Alma to meet who had a lot of pull with the police and local government, so they were passed through quickly.

From the Caribbean to David, which is near the Pacific, showed lush jungles and few settlements. Volcan Barú is near, and was quite imposing. Dave had collected a lot of plants on the volcano and in the mountains between Chiriqui Grande, on the Caribbean, and David. He flew over the road to see the dam, which was a major spot where Dave had explored the first few years he was in the country. There were peaks as high as eighteen hundred meters.

Alma said she was sure she was going to like Panamá! It was beautiful, and they hadn't seen one city! Chiriqui Grande was a little fishing village!

They could see David wasn't like large cities, though it was second largest in Panamá. It was spread out.

There were a few fairly tall buildings, but not a clutter of ugly high-rises or any of that. Dave had said, often, that it was a great big puebla. It has casinos and fine restaurants and malls and other trappings, but managed to stay more of a town.

The people they met, with one exception, were friendly and curious. Alma was the center of attention as soon as she got off the jet, as always. She was a spectacular woman.

Dave was waiting with a well-built man CD would estimate to be fifty five to sixty years old. He looked a bit familiar. He was introduced as Clint Faraday.

"I've seen you somewhere before?" CD asked.

"Sarasota. Nineteen eighty eight. That NASA deal. Warne."

"That's twenty four years, so I'm a bit vague. You worked for the man in, where was it? Toward the center of the state and south?"

"I was checking up on the ex-wife, who turned out to be the biggest of the crooks. You used my testimony in her trial."

"But you were about forty five years old then! You can't be much over that now!"

"I'm sixty nine. Life is good here and you don't age so fast.

"I can see what Dave meant when he said he wanted my wife to come. There would be the two most beautiful women in the world! He was right!"

"How sweet!" Alma cried. "That Indian girl Dave sent pictures of? She can't be ... oh, yes. He said you married her and that you have two children."

"She's twenty eight. I'm declared a Ngobe and she's Ngobe."

"I can picture you, Tyna and Shirley Jacobi here. The world would never be the same!" Dave said. "Selma's got your rooms ready.

"I figure we can go to La Fortuna tomorrow and to the comarca in three days. We can stop in Cusapín for the night so you can meet Tyna and the kids. We can look over my collection there, then head to the wilds. I figured you'd rather go to places no one's ever been who knew the difference between and oak tree and an orchid."

"Didn't I tell you?" Alma said to CD, who grinned and nodded.

"Those boys are Indios," Alma said. "You said they're handsome. You're right."

"These are in the city too much. They're not like the comarca and mountain Indios. Those are gods next to these," Dave replied.

"Are these gay?" Alma asked. "They seem to spend a lot of time hugging each other!"

Clint laughed. "I don't think they're gay. We Ngobe touch a lot. I hug them and they hug me. It doesn't go beyond that – with me. I understand Dave takes it further sometimes."

"Oh, yeah! That's another difference in here and the states," Dave said. "We look at things from a different cultural perspective. I'm among them most of the time and live in their culture, which beats ours handsdown!

"Let's get to the house. You'll be tired from the

flight.

"How's JK? Still running the whole world with his comps?"

"We all wish he could, but that's gotten awfully complicated," CD answered. They talked about politics and such as they loaded the car and headed for Dave's rented house not very far from the airport.

Alma was as beautiful a woman as Tyna. She was a normal woman, like Tyna. A couple of times Alma said, "CD!" when he started to give orders. Dave said he was used to running huge corporations and had fifty people around ready to jump when he wanted anything. Alma was trying to break him of the habit. Just tell him to fuck off if he gave you any orders. Other than that, he seemed like a very good person.

"CD's used to having people jump because he's got so much money. He mostly ignores them, but it can get you into a bad habit," Alma said. "It's also his method with the detective thing. He goes into a case knowing that he *will* solve it. He can seem to be overbearing at times, but it works.

"My God! I don't think I want to drive here!"

Several taxis and two SUVs were jockeying for position. It looked like there would be a five car pileup, but they managed to avoid actually hitting each other.

"Hah! This is nothing! Panamá City is an open

demolition derby!" Dave said. "I always say the taxi drivers have to get a certificate from asshole school to hold a license here, but that's true of taxi drivers the world over.

"We can rest awhile, then I'll treat you to a meal at La Tipica. I know you like shrimp, and theirs is the best!"

"I'm paying for the food. No argument!" CD said.

"In the states, their shrimp plate would cost on the order of thirty five dollars a plate. Here, it's eight fifty," Clint said. "I'll pick you up at six?"

They agreed, but CD said they would take taxis. He heard they weren't so expensive here, either.

"From my place? Stand by the bus stop and you get a ride for sixty cents apiece to downtown. The Pedregal bus is thirty five cents. You can walk from my place to Las Brasas, which would be my second choice. Unbelievable rib-eye steak! Same price. It would cost sixty bucks in the states!"

"The bus is only thirty five cents? What? Three blocks? Where is Pedregal?" Alma asked.

"Pedregal is across from the airport. Downtown is about five kilometers, I think. The marina at Pedregal is as far as the bus goes. Maybe seven kilometers. The bus is thirty five cents if you want to go one block or the whole distance," Dave explained. "Taxis are generally a dollar and a quarter to a dollar and a half. They take people to

Pedregal and would return empty except for carrying passengers for sixty cents apiece. They generally carry five, so that's three dollars, the same as the trip from downtown to Pedregal. Panamá has a very good transportation system and the best roads in Central America."

"I can say that everything you've said about this places is exactly as you said it is," Alma said happily. "I already love the places and haven't been anywhere except at an airport and riding in a car!"

"It gets to you fast," Dave said. "I'll tell you about my first trip here someday!"

"You already did," she replied with an impish grin. "Like fifty times!"

"Here we are. See you at sixish," Clint said.

CD looked at the house and said, "This is what you pay three hundred a month for?"

"Uh-huh."

"In Florida it would be fifteen hundred plus maintenance plus electric, plus anything else."

"I do pay electric."

"How much?"

"Twenty one twelve."

"Sheesh!"

They went inside where Selma greeted them. She and Alma got into a discussion of the changes in Florida and Panamá over the past few years since Selma moved there.

"You live here with Dave. I like this place!

"I suppose he spends most of his time in the jungles."

"I spend some time here, even when Dave is gone. I have my own place near Las Tablas. You'll love that place, too."

They talked a lot about people. Alma said there seemed to be as many fat people there as the states anymore. Selma explained that a lot of the men liked bigger women. Out of the city there weren't so many.

They spent the next two days in the mountains, researching orchids.

"Oh, Nick! I was thinking I would hate this place from what we went through in Panamá City! This is really different and really nice, isn't it?" Janet Storie said to Nick as they went to get a taxi from Malek Airport in David, Panamá. "We flew over miles and miles of pure jungle! I thought it would be hot. Everyone said David is hot, but this is comfortable! Naples is easily ten degrees hotter, and without a breeze! It's exactly what Dave said in his e-mails.

"I wish we could have gotten in touch with him before we came. I'd like to see him. He's about seventy five now, so probably doesn't get around like he used to.

"I have the phone number he sent four or five years ago, but he's probably moved by now. I would have to know the area code."

Nick laughed. Janet was excited. "I think the whole country is one area code, so all you'd have to do is dial the number. I'm sure it's changed by now, but you could try. What can it cost? A quarter?

They went out the door to the airport to flag a taxi. One came up and they put their bags in and got in. They said, "Where is a good medium-priced hotel?" He said the Best Western. Rooms from about fifty dollars. The taxi was six dollars.

"Oh! We know a man here! He told us about David! He says he knows a lot of people. They call him Dave. He has very white hair and..." Janet began.

"He runs around with Clint Faraday? That Dave? Plays the guitar and writes books?"

"Yes, that would be Dave!"

"I'll take you to the Alcalá. Nice, and thirty bucks double. Taxi's two bucks. Dave's a friend. He's done favors for my family. Clint, too."

"Do you know where we can find him?"

"He might be here or he might be in the jungle somewhere. Mostly, it's in the jungle."

"I have a phone number, but it's five years old or more, so I don't suppose he has it anymore."

"He has it. He has a cheap cell he bought when he first came here and it still works. He had several expensive ones in between that don't work."

"Oh! I'll call him then! You say it's a cell phone?"

"Most of them are anymore. Lots of Blackberry and lots of those computer types. His is an old one. You can use mine."

He handed her his cellular."

"How kind! Thank you!" She punched the

number and the call button. Nothing happened. She asked what she'd done wrong.

"You say the number was more than five years ago?"

"Yes."

"Add a six in front. They changed to where cell numbers begin with six."

She tried that. It rang three times, then Dave answered.

"Dave! Where are you? This is Janet. Janet Storie!"

"Janet? It's good to hear from you. It's been more than a couple of years, hasn't it? How is Nick and the kids?"

"We're all fine. Nick and I are on vacation. We're in David!"

"Really?! Why didn't you call me and let me know you were coming? Selma's here with me, and CD and Alma just came in an hour ago! I think we ... yes! We have an unused guest room! Come here! I insist, so no shit!"

"Where are you? We're just leaving the airport in a taxi. The driver knows you and this is his phone."

"Let me talk to him. You're about a mile from my place."

Janet handed the phone to the driver. They talked a minute, then he said they'd be right there. He looked around and took a side road after another minute and pulled up in front of a rather nice large house with a steel grate fence. Nick said Dave was doing very well, indeed! The books must be selling. That place had to cost a grand a month, even though Panamá prices were a lot less than Florida. Maintenance and maid service cost ... no, Selma was there. Expensive, no matter what.

"I think about three hundred a month. It *is* expensive, but it's a big house," the driver said.

Dave came out the gate with a woman who looked familiar. She was probably a movie star or something. Nothing surprised them with Dave.

Selma came out with them, then a man he recognized, CD Grimes. The woman must be his wife. She was supposed to be a beauty, and this one was certainly that!

CD chatted with the driver, who took the bags out of the trunk and Nick paid him. It was a dollar and a quarter. They didn't go all the way to downtown. Nick gave him two dollars and they went to the house. Selma, CD and Alma were waiting on the porch and were introduced.

"Nick Storie. I've heard a lot about you. JK and Tony and Shirley are friends."

"We go places together now and then. To Jim's place on the island out of Naples. We all go to concerts sometimes. The guys from Not So Hard Times play the area, so we all go. Lonnie goes with us a lot, and Serena, his wife.

"I guess you've heard of Lonnie Micks."

"He's as beautiful a man as exists," Janet said. "They had a baby who's going to be so handsome it scares you!"

Alma and Selma agreed. Alma said she was sick of hearing man talk, so the girls would go inside and gossip about them.

"We're going to head for the mountains in a couple of days," Dave said. "CD is an orchid nut. I don't think you're interested in them, are you, Nick?"

"Not really. I think they're pretty, but I'm not into flowers.

"Janet and I have a free vacation on a big mobster, so we thought we'd come here where you said it's so perfect."

"Which one?" Dave asked.

"Artie Doniletti. He and Greco insisted. We're to watch the budget and not to spend more than a million a week."

"Doniletti? I've had some contact with him. He's not the big bad mobster he used to be. The bunch have gone pretty much legit," CD said. "He did the country a favor when he got the Comptons out of Georgia!"

"Yes. Pancho was behind that," Nick agreed.

"How is Pancho?" Dave asked. "I've lost touch with a lot of the people from Florida. We still communicate about three times a year."

"He's a proud father for the second time. He's a very popular figure in South Florida."

"Pancho DeGullio? The most powerful drug lord in the world until you showed he did it all on bluff?" CD asked, grinning.

"He's still the most powerful person in the world when it comes to mobs. They're scared shitless of him!" Dave said.

They talked for another hour, then Clint came by to be introduced. He and Nick seemed to hit it off as well as he and CD had.

Nick was an observer. He was damned good at analyzing a person. CD was sure of himself to an extent that sometimes crossed the line into arrogance. Clint was more a "Go with the flow" type. Nick had been forced, in a few of his cases, to be pragmatic. CD was more the type who would solve a case and pass the responsibility to the courts or whatever. Dave was in some other world.

Nick Storie was a lucky man. He had the best wife in the world and a job he loved and two kids people considered geniuses (he didn't) and was able to make friends with even the world's most powerful mobsters, as well as with almost anybody else who would meet him half way.

If this country was as Dave explained he was really going to enjoy this vacation.

Clint got on his boat three days later. CD, Alma, Nick and Janet – along with Dave and Selma, of course – were going to spend the night with him in Cusapín, then Dave, CD and Alma were off for the jungle. Nick and Janet were going to stay with Clint and family for a few days. Selma would go to Bocas Town.

They were all delighted with the place. Miles of beautiful Caribbean sand beaches, rain forests, beautiful water, beautiful view, beautiful people who were warm and friendly. Nito and Nicole came to greet them from the house and to help carry their things. They were introduced and Janet said they were as handsome as Lonnie's kids. CD, Alma, Selma and Nick knew what she was talking about, as did Dave, who said they would see why in a minute. Selma grinned.

They went to the house, where Tyna was laying out a delicious feast of native dishes. She was a stunningly beautiful woman. Indio, with long thick shiny hair to below her waist.

While Janet was far more than an average beautiful woman, Alma was blond and, as Dave stated, one of the most beautiful women in the world. The contrast with the dark woman who was one of the most beautiful women in the world was startling.

They immediately decided they were friends. All of them. They chatted in Spanish and English and were surprised that Nito and Nicole spoke almost unaccented English as well as perfect Spanish and Ngobe. They could shift from one to the other with ease. Dave, Selma and Nick could speak almost as well, except Nick didn't know Ngobe, of course, but preferred to stay with one language, as did Selma. They would have to stop to consider words when they were mixed. CD spoke some Spanish, but was not fluent.

They went around the town and the area. Alma kept finding orchids she'd never seen, as did CD. Nick and Janet couldn't care less about orchids, but were fascinated with the thousands of parrots and two kinds of monkeys. They took a lot of pictures of people and the area. CD said he was glad he brought two dozen memory chips for the cameras. They were going to fill one 8 gig chip before they left Cusapín!

Two little boys and a little girl, all about five or six years old, came along the beach and were greeted. Nito brought them to the house to be introduced. After about twenty minutes they said they were going to go back home. They had been curious about the gringas. Everybody said there was one who was blond and as beautiful as a movie star, most of whom were ugly, except for the makeup and false boobs. Tyna knew the joke, Alma looked a little surprised and nervous, Janet caught it pretty fast. Selma winked at Tyna.

"They're saying you're actually beautiful, while movie stars have to paint on the beauty. It's because none of us wear makeup, isn't it?"

"Yes," Tyna replied. "Only the whores in Chiriqui Grande wear makeup. It makes them look artificial."

"But these are only children! What do they know of whores?" Alma asked.

"They know about life and people and nature," Clint explained. "Where in the United States would three five and six year old kids be walking alone on a beach – or even in a park – a kilometer from home?"

"There are perverts in any society," CD warned. "They can't always control themselves."

"Not here," Tyna said.

"How can you be sure?" CD asked.

"Because they'd be dead," Nicole answered. "They don't get counseling and excuses here."

"I read about that in some of Dave's books," Nick put in. "After you're of age, you do what you want. Until then, it's the strongest law on the comarca."

"Yeah! I have to wait until I'm twelve to get

molested! Bummer!" Nicole said. "I wish I was a boy. They can get molested anytime they say it's alright."

Nick was amused. Dave, Selma, Tyna and Clint didn't seem to pay any attention to it. Alma and CD were shocked. Janet seemed mildly surprised.

"So you're the one in the states who bought one of my books!" Dave said. "You been screwed yet, Nito? You're nine, so you should be having a little fun now and then."

"I didn't like it. I mean, it wasn't bad, but I don't like it. Santos and Rubio like it. I suppose when I'm on the other end of the stick I'll like it."

"Santos and Rubio are your age?" CD asked.

"No. Santos is eleven and Rubio is twelve. They can get off. At least, Rubio can. I don't know about Santos, but he's more gay."

"I don't believe we're having this kind of crazy conversation!" Alma cried. "Clint, he's your *son*! You don't even seem concerned that he was raped?!"

"I wasn't raped. Ton ... a friend wanted to and I wanted to see what it was like, so I said okay. I didn't like it and he only did it one other time when we were playing and it was part of the game, so I agreed by getting in the game."

"They know more about sex at six than I did at sixty," Clint said. "Everyone's done that kind of thing. They just don't lie about it here. They know it's part of growing up.

"If someone actually raped one of my kids they'd die a very slow and horrendous death, I guarantee."

"CD is probably the only male here who was never molested, but he had a unique life. His grandfather was one of the most famous private detectives in the states and his great grandfather was a billionaire. If anyone touched him they had no chance of surviving more than a couple of hours," Dave said. "Until I came here there weren't ten people who knew half the things I did except the ones I did it with. Here, so what? I'm no different than most of them."

"You've never denied that you tend to be bi," Selma said. "I think I'll go back to Las Tablas tomorrow when you go wandering off in the jungle. I was going to Bocas, but it'll be so cheap and gaudy after here."

Selma had a nice place in Las Tablas, on the Pacific. The conversation changed to other things and they sacked out about midnight.

In the morning they decided to go their separate ways, so everyone crowded into Clint's boat to head for Chiriqui Grande. They would spend an hour or so there, then CD, Alma, Dave and Selma would take Clint's car to David. Nick and Janet would go back to Cusapín.

They were almost to the docks in Chiriqui when

Clint got a call. Tyna answered and said it was their old friend from Bocas, Sergio.

"Yo, Sergio! You're back in Bocas or still in David?"

"Bocas. Clint, I don't have much time, but there's a murder that I want to ask your help with. It's out of my league, what with gringos and Germans and Canadians mixed up in it."

It was on speaker. Dave smirked and said this was a great time to find a puzzling murder!

"Who was that? Dave?" Sergio asked. "This is weird enough for him!"

"I'm almost to Chiriqui Grande now. I have company, but I'll try to get to Bocas. I'll call when I grab a bus."

"What the hell?!" Dave exploded. "Take your car! *We'll* take a bus! Christ!"

"You've never seen Bocas, so we can take an extra day and all go there," Clint suggested.

"Tyna will go back home. Selma and I will take a bus. The rest can go to Bocas in Clint's car," Dave suggested.

"I'll go back to Cusapín with Tyna," Janet said. "I've spent as much time as I care to in Key West, and everyone says Bocas Town is just like Key West."

They agreed to that. Clint said he would be there soon. He was going to take Janet and Tyna to Cusapín, Dave and Selma would take the car, and he would take the boat to Bocas with a couple of famous detectives. The three of them should be able to solve a little murder in two minutes!

They tied to the dock. Omar was there and was going back to Cusapín in a couple of hours. Janet had never been in a cayuca, so Tyna would take her with Omar and Clint and Nick and CD and Alma could go on to Bocas in the boat.

"I've had enough of Key West, myself," Alma said. "I think I'll go with Dave and Selma to David. I like it there. If you get tied up with a case here I can go with Dave to look for orchids. It's what I'm here for!"

"We can go to Fortuna in the areas we didn't go to the past couple of days. It's been a couple of years and I'd like to see what's changed up there," Dave agreed. "So! You three master detectives can divide your murder into three parts and see who solves it."

Clint tied to the police dock to ask for Sergio, who wasn't there. He would be back in an hour or so. Clint went around to his place on Saigon Bay. He was tying to his deck when his next door neighbor, Judi Lum, a very attractive Oriental woman who was the best person Clint ever found for getting information, came onto her dock. He introduced everyone and found that Judi hadn't been able to learn anything about the murder. It was a man from Belgium, Hans Borker. He had been killed back by Sixth Street. They thought it was a mugging, but nothing fit. All she heard was that a couple of Canadians and two gringos and a German had some kind of deal that they were arguing about. They all seemed to hate each other and everyone was blaming everyone else for their problems.

"They kept mentioning the tongs, so I imagine they crossed Mama Chiang and are in hot water."

Mama Chiang was the reputed head of the most powerful tong in Panamá. She lived on Isla Colón out past the bluffs in a big house on the water where illegal Chinese were suspected of being brought in.

"Damn!" Clint said. "Sergio didn't say the Chinese were involved! That makes it mean and probably unsolvable!"

"Oh, he doesn't know. I heard that while I was talking with Travis and Yveth."

That was Judi's value. She innocently talked about things with people and would drop a word or name in passing, act like she couldn't care less, and would get all kinds of information it would take days for Clint to find. He probably would never have learned the Chinese were involved without that!

"I'd like to dig a bit for you, but I have to be in Santiago tonight, so it's up to you."

She had a taxi waiting, so left.

"Seems we're on our own with something I'd have avoided if I'd known," Clint complained.

"It does make it interesting," Nick replied.

"I can get information about anything through my links with Crane," CD said. "They'll have a lot about your tong in the military files."

"No. We do this on our own. The last thing we want is for the states to intrude here more than they have," Clint said. "They get a hint and we'll have CIA and God knows who here fucking up things. The voice of experience speaks!"

"I can get information through the mobs, but I'll agree," Nick said.

"I have a few connections with the mobs," Clint said. "They're not in the states.

"We're on our own!"

The three detectives went to the station to speak with Sergio Valdez, the head of the police in Bocas. He met the others and said he'd had a couple of conversations with a Jim Hill and a Marsha Blevins in Naples through the police computer lines. Dave had suggested it. He had also once talked with JK on a special cellular Dave carried to learn how to get something from a locked computer. He'd even talked with a man who was supposed to be the most powerful mob boss in the world, Pancho DeGulio, on that phone!

"It seems Dave knows about everybody," Sergio said. "He's not impressed by money, but will knock himself out if someone wants to help people. Deserving people, not bums because they want to be bums.

"What we have is that a man was killed back by Sixth Street, just across on C. Hans Borker. Brest Belgium. He's traveling with five people who are in some kind of business deal. They refuse any information, but I hear they were asking about purchasing land on the water out from town. More toward Drago.

"They don't seem to like each other.

"There are two from Canada, Robert Healey and Keith Stoner. Alberta.

"There are two from the states. George Billings and Harry Stine. Galveston and Los Angeles.

"There is one from Germany Gustav Kroner. Hamburg.

"They have been here for less than a week. They were arguing a lot, but no one knows what the subject of the arguments were. They argued in German.

"I've checked as much as I can in the time. Borker was involved with some kind of illegal importation in Germany. Healey and Stoner were in a tourist ship deal between Canada and Japan. Billings and Stoner were in farming in California and Texas.

"Kroner, there's no information. It may be an alias and he might carry a false passport. If it is, it's good! Maybe an altered stolen passport.

"He was killed with a garrote, but was also stabbed in the left side. Nothing was removed from the body that we have learned of.

"That's what we have."

"Okay. Sixth Street and behind are the bad part of Bocas Town," Clint said. "There are a number of people living there who came from Colón. I think you'll know what Colón is."

"Transportation and farming. They're moving something," Nick suggested. "Colón? I'd say drugs."

"No evidence of such," Sergio replied.

"Whatever," CD said. "I heard of some uranium being smuggled out of here a couple of years ago."

"It's tied in with agriculture, as a guess," Nick argued. "That would be drugs, first, or something that it would be illegal to take out."

"A new orchid species?" CD wondered. "That *Phragmipedium kovachii* from Peru would have made several people millionaires if they hadn't been caught. Dave's discovered several new species here and there's *bessae* that's very much on that order here. He found a *Sobralia* that's new. *Scaphyglottis* and *Epidendrums*.

"You have *Encyclia cordigera* here. If it was discovered in this day and age it would be worth millions."

"Dave discovered an *Anthurium* that got a few people shot. He was almost one of them," Sergio said. "Believe it or not, those people would kill each other for the right to name the thing!"

"He sent Alma a couple of seeds. We have them growing in the intermediate house," CD said, nodding in agreement. "I have an idea for an approach to this. Let's spend a day or two, each with his own method. We can find what's behind it and go from there. If we establish motive we should have it pretty well solved."

They all agreed. Clint and Sergio would fill Nick and CD in on local things. He took them to the Golden Grill and introduced them to several of the local characters. They went their own ways from there.

CD left the Golden Grill and went to the house to use Clint's computer to contact JK, in Florida. He gave the names of everyone he'd heard about to that point. JK grunted and said he's send to that address as soon as he had anything.

A handsome man named Ben Longstreet came in while he was working. He said he heard Clint was back. He kept an eye on the place for him. He watered the plants when Judi was away.

He didn't know anything except that a tourist was murdered. He didn't get involved in Clint's cases. That could be dangerous.

JK sent that Borker was Borker. He didn't have any information on record because he never did anything. He arranged for people to get jobs internationally the past few years. It was all done through the comps. Mostly higher-end engineers and so forth, but he would handle anything from common labor in the oil fields to cruise ship personnel to business management and up.

Healy and Stoner were into cruise lines and had made some shady deals with second-rate cruises posing as prime.

That could be a connection.

Billings and Stine did contracted agricultural work. They employed a lot of Mexicans and Guatemalans, a percent of whom were illegal and they knew it.

Stine had once gotten involved with a Chinese ring who were suspected of bringing young girls into California and forcing them into prostitution. He left California and went to Texas, where he seemed legit, if not liked.

He thought for a minute, then called Sergio and said to get him some passport information and send it to him at Clint's house. He needed it right away.

"No," Sergio replied.

"What?"

"That's information that's not in your province to get from me."

"I need it! It could answer a very hard question or two!"

"And?"

"I don't...?"

"I'm supposed to tell you to go fuck yourself if you give orders," Sergio answered, with a laugh.

CD laughed. "I do that! How about if I request some passport information?"

"You're at Clint's house. Turn on his computer and go to section three. It's Section PP. It's a direct secure connection. I'll send the things we've received. (CD went to the section on the computer.)

"I was speaking with Sheriff Stewart. He said you're fully qualified and are a deputy in his department and a special state marshal for the grand jury, which you don't believe in. You're used to giving orders. I'm to tell you to fuck off when you do. You don't get bent."

"You called Florida?"

"I check on anyone involved in these things. Clint taught me that!

"Stewart said to tell you your son, another CD, is working for him while he gets his degree, as you know, and that he has solved a case for him. He's not as big-headed about it as you always are."

The information came onto the screen. They chatted a minute more and CD rang off and studied the information.

Borker was somehow the key, he was sure.

Born in Dulange, Belgium. Attended university in Brest, Belgium. Business management major. Studied criminology as minor. Worked for Silas Dupont one year. Disappeared until two months ago, when he had his passport certified? Silas Dupont?

CD had heard of Silas Dupont. Borker had been an Interpol agent.

Vedddyy inderesdink! He had gotten in with this bunch as an undercover agent, so they were up to something big.

Interpol wasn't into agriculture or drugs to any extent. They were more art and jewelry ... and there was all that pirate treasure coming from Panamá lately! Clint Faraday was in on a lot of it. That museum on the comarca was eleven billion dollars!

He wanted to discuss a thing or three with Clint!

Nick spoke with people at the Golden Grill. Clint and CD soon left and he stayed. Jim was a very interesting person.

Jim said there was something strange and a bit sinister about the whole group where Borker was concerned. They were partners in something that was stepping on the wrong kind of toes.

"I don't know what it is, but that Boko character seems very interested in them. He's one of Mama Chiang's men.

"She's reputed to be the head of the tongs here. I wouldn't doubt it.

"Uh-oh. Here comes Tom. Clint despises him. He's one of those people who have some kind of need to top your story, no matter what. He's going to know everything there is to know about the case and he knows everyone involved. It's total bullshit. We let him hang around for amusement. He gets into traps he made."

Nick grinned and nodded. He was introduced to Tom as a cop from Florida.

"What part of Florida? I worked with the police in Tampa for awhile. Investigative department."

"Naples. Homicide."

"Oh, really? Do you know Bill Angeles there? Head of something or other. Worked with him in Tampa before he was transferred."

"Never heard of him except some article in the Police Gazette. We get a kick out of those phony stories they make up."

"Er, ah. Yes. He was embarrassed by all that. I was only there for a few days, so don't know what was going on.

"We have a second rate detective from there living right here. Clint Faraday. Gets involved with the police and interferes with their work, then claims it was him who solved something."

"Clint? I'm staying at his places here. He's respected all over the world. He's a lot of things, but you're the first I ever heard who called him second rate. Sergio can't say enough good about him! Same was true in David. Tonio, head of violent crimes unit, said Clint solved a couple of things for him."

He was trying to think of everyone Clint and Dave had mentioned.

"Silvio, in Chitre, said he really got a big one solved there. It ended up with him getting a million dollars or something. Basilio, jefe on the comarca, says anything they get, they turn over to him because he's practical and thinks like the rest of his people.

"Clint's proud to be declared a Ngobe because of

all he's done for them.

"How can you call anyone like that second rate?"

"Oh, no! It's a joke between us! He says I'm a pain in the ass and I say he's second rate! It's just a joke!"

"Well, he's right, at least," Jim said. "Why didn't you ever tell us about Tampa?"

"Er, I, uh, hmm."

"I'd like to chat, but I'm helping Sergio with that Borker murder," Nick said. "Some vacation! It's like I showed up at the station on time this morning for an assignment!"

"Oh, yes. That guy who crossed his partners or something. I'd think that one was cut and dried! One or all of them did it!"

"Oh, probably. I have to establish motive. These kinds of things are usually among people from the same place who know each other. That's that little weird group. I have to find what they're up to."

"Setting up money laundering for the mafia in California. I'd think that was obvious," Tom said, condescendingly.

"Then why the two from Canada and the German?" Nick asked.

"Er. Spread it out so no one suspects. That's why they always argue. So us people will think they're not working together."

"And why is Boko getting into it?" Jim asked.

"Why, er, Boko? Because Mama Chiang wants

to run all that.”

“Mama Chiang is into laundering?” Jim asked. “That’s news! Smith and Niko were arguing with that Stine person. They’re all tangled with Mama Chiang.”

“Anders, too,” Tom said, leaning closer across the table. “I saw them day before yesterday on the ferry dock when it came in. I was wondering why they were all there. I think, now this is a guess, there was something that came in on that ferry that they all wanted.

“See, if they had some kind of shipment that Mama Chiang found out about, she would be the one to try to grab it.

“I do know they almost got into it!”

Jim nodded the least bit at Nick. “I heard about that. It was them and Mama Chiang’s boys? Not them and Anders?”

“Anders wasn’t even there by then! He was sitting in the Pirate when I went by ten minutes later!”

Jim raised an eyebrow and nodded. This was actual information.

The subject changed and Nick said he had to go.

He had something, but what was it?

He went to the China to get some things for the house. He looked around at the stores and noted they were all Chinese. He remembered walking past several stores. All the food stores and a lot of the other almacenes were owned by the Chinese!

He walked up and down all the streets of Bocas Town and out to Saigon Bay. All the food stores were Chinese. Most of the restaurants were Chinese.

Nick thought, just maybe, Mama Chiang was a lot more than a bystander.

Clint grinned as he left the Golden Grill. Tom was waiting in the park for him to go so he could go over and make a big impression on the gringo. Nick was going to get more information about everybody than he could believe, and all of it bullshit.

Well, Jim would warn him.

He went to the station to ask about the people, knowing Sergio would have all that the police network could find about them. While he was there he found that CD was at the house using the computer when he called Sergio. He told Sergio to tell him to fuck off if he got orders. He listened to Sergio's end of the conversation and read the information being sent. He came to the same conclusion CD had about Interpol, so called Manolo, an agent for that and a couple of other international police agencies. All he found was that Borker wasn't working with art, jewels or drugs.

He contacted Manny Matthews, actually Marko Bocinni, a major mob boss from California who had gone legitimate and was living on Isla San Cristóbal where he could raise a family who wouldn't be ashamed of what Pops did to get his money, even though it was Manny's father who ran the mob like a mob.

The story was that Bocinni was living on a private island in the Mediterranean. He handled the business through computers. He was still powerful and could get information no one else could.

Borker, nothing.

Healey, a few cheap cons.

Stoner, ditto.

Billings, ditto.

Stine, ditto, except he tried to get into prostitution with the wrong group in California. Manny had been "instrumental" in closing down the connections to China.

Kroner was a question mark, but was probably just a schmuck who never did anything to get attention of anybody.

They certainly weren't into money laundering. That was ridiculous. They had no more than a bare minimum financing, none from anyone who would need another laundering scheme.

Judi said they had some kind of argument with Boko. He was muscle for Mama Chiang and wouldn't have connections with anyone from anywhere else, so what was that about?

"Clint, Esteban said he saw Anders talking with Niko and Boko and Kroner. That could mean something. They seemed to be arguing. Anders was heard to say someone was going to end up fish bait."

"I've heard one tale too many about Mama Chiang's boys. I think I'll go talk to Anders. He's on and off with Chiang, so maybe he'll let something slip.

"I just can't picture anything where Mama Chiang and that bunch could be getting at cross purposes because of ... or maybe I can! But *how*?"

He decided to look up Anders, who ran a sort of half-assed water taxi that catered to private deals. He would bring in people who weren't supposed to be there and no one would know they were there, where the legitimate taxis took the required ID information.

Anders had a little office that was on the porch of his house on Fifth Street. He would loan money at eight percent – per week. He would lend you ten percent value on cameras and cell phones and computers. If it was found they were stolen, it wasn't his fault! He wasn't required to ask for receipts on personal items, such as the nine cell phones a local bum brought to him. If three were reported stolen, he would be very happy to return them to the owners! He wasn't a fence! He would make the bum return any of the money he hadn't drunk up yet.

That way he got nine fifty dollar cell phones for thirty bucks. He returned three of them, so he had three hundred bucks that he spent thirty dollars on.

"Heard you had a row with that bunch of wannabe something-or-others," Clint said, after chatting for a minute about the less than average surfer bunch this year. Clint said too many were getting ripped off for cameras and phones and computers and wouldn't come back anymore. It was getting as bad as Costa Rica.

"Phftt! Never-will-bes. Idiots! Think they can bring in girls and open a casino on maybe ten thousand dollars. The damned license for the casino would be fifty grand! Idiots!"

"They want to run girls? None of the guys here would give them a second look!"

"Gringas and Suizas and Alemanias. They think anyone here would pay those prices when you can get a girl on the street for fifteen? Idiots!"

"Amos said they wanted to get their hands on old Indio pottery and such, and pirate treasure, but everyone thinks there's an unending source of pirate treasure here."

"There is for the comarca! More than ten billion dollars worth! I wish I could figure a way to get my hands on a few little things. I could retire!"

"Yeah. They went to all the places on the maps and found out that most of it was found a long time ago. Most of it was in other places. If it wasn't for the international publicity it got this government would send in soldiers and take it."

"Yeah. They say I'm a corrupt crook. Didn't they look at the damned government here? I'm an amateur!"

They chatted for a minute more, then Clint went to the ferry dock. Smith was there. He was a big black who did things for anyone who would pay.

He refused to talk. Period.

CD, Nick and Clint met at his house just before sundown. Earl and Ben came with food. They were neighbors and good friends and were chefs for gourmets.

After eight o'clock Earl and Ben went into town and the three detectives sat to compare what they had found.

Borker was an agent for Interpol. He wasn't working on jewels, art, drugs or anything else Interpol specialized in. It was probable that the others had tumbled and he died as a result.

They had no idea what the bunch was up to. It didn't have anything to do with artifacts or pirate treasure, except as a possible sideline for one or two of them.

They weren't connected. It wasn't about money laundering, but could have been. The idea was to open a casino and launder through it the same as hundreds were doing already. They would be crowded or run out of that in a week.

There might be some connection with Mama Chiang, but she wasn't into laundering money, except through what was an obvious ruse.

Healey and Stoner were in moving people, but

that could translate into cargo on cruise ships.

Billings is a nobody with some agricultural ties. Stine is, too, but was caught in a scheme to bring in prostitutes. Check on that. There was a hint of that kind of thing.

Kroner was a big question mark.

"Okay. That's general and overall. Now we add our little finds to it," Clint suggested. "I found that Mama Chiang is definitely involved somehow."

"I see a possible connection to something that would explain the agricultural end and possibly even the transportation end," CD said. "I had a couple of cases that were based on genetically engineered things. One was poisonous plants and one was about foods that could be grown in salt water.

"I don't suppose that would be here, though. A scientist and the military in the states were behind the first case and Israelis were behind the second. Zionists."

"I've had a case where genetic insertions were used," Clint said. "It could be, but I don't see how that could include others."

"I think maybe it's a scheme to get your pirate ship's treasures, somehow," Nick said. "Not really, but it's the only suggestion I've had that makes sense."

"When we add it up, it contains agriculture, Interpol and transportation," Clint said. "There's something we don't have."

"It also contains Mama Chiang. We have to find everything she's into to know where the real truth lies," Nick argued. "I can't help but think she's behind all the rest.

"What's she into, Clint?"

"Well, her reputation is that she imports a lot of Chinese. They get off the boat with permanent resident status and open small businesses. She's managed to take control of the food markets in a big portion of ... and there it is!"

"Yes! It has to be!" CD cried.

"I think I agree," Nick said. "So. Let's add it up with that equation.

"The bunch uses transportation and Interpol about like we thought. We were looking at the agricultural part as being agricultural, but it was about getting workers.

"They were planning to set up a deal where they got people, probably mostly women, here with an indenture scheme. Stine was caught up in that kind of thing in California ten years ago and managed to slip out of it. Healey was getting Mexican and Guatemalan illegals jobs.

"Kroner has connections where European and Asian people who are desperate could be used in such a scheme. In higher income positions."

"And Mama Chiang is running that kind of thing. It would interfere with her scheme," CD agreed.

"Borker was about to expose the thing, which would also give Mama Chiang publicity that could shut part of her things down," Clint added. "Now we have to learn who killed Borker. That puts us in a scary position. We're against these amateurs on one side and the tong on the other.

"In the morning I'm going calling on Mama Chiang."

"I'll go calling on the people she was using here," CD said.

"And I'll go calling on our plotters. Particularly the one I think was the brains. Kroner."

They relaxed and had a couple beers. CD asked if Ben was gay.

"Ben? Yes. Both of them. They're a couple. Why?" Clint answered.

"I just wondered. They seem affectionate with each other. I'm getting used to the guys hugging each other and such, but they seemed closer than that."

They discussed the difference in the cultures and sacked out around midnight.

In the morning Clint headed for The Bluffs and Mama Chiang. Niko met him at the gate and said Mama Chiang was expecting him. He went in and was ushered to the veranda where she was having breakfast. She invited him to join her. He said he'd eaten, but could always use a cup of coffee.

"Well, Mr. Faraday. I've been expecting you since Smith said you asked some questions he wouldn't answer."

"They were about him, not you. The fact he came to you answers some of the questions. I was coming because your name and organization were mentioned by a number of people."

She nodded. "My organization?"

"It's simply common knowledge. We don't need to dance around about it. You're offering employment to people who wouldn't have any, otherwise. I may not approve of the fact you make more than they do off of it, but there are probably any number of things about me you wouldn't be able to approve.

"Do you know who Borker was?"

"The dead man? He was an accountant of some sort, according to my sources."

"Then you'd better find better sources. He was Interpol. If you were behind his murder, you've brought an international investigation on that you can't bribe or intimidate."

She stared hard at him for a moment. "I see.

"No, Mr. Faraday, I was not behind his killing. If I were, there would be no body and the crabs several miles out in the Caribbean would be well-fed for awhile.

"I cannot say that no one close to me was involved. That kind of thing can happen when a person thinks he is doing a favor for another person. The road to Hell is cobbled with good intentions.

"Mr. Faraday, I've been greatly curtailed in the import department by the recent amnesty program that showed some people had carried improper identification. We are an intelligent people and they saw they could have amnesty and become truly legal here, meanwhile relieving themselves of paying for being here in the first place. I have had to virtually cease the operation.

"It isn't all negative. I can use a little retirement to rest and enjoy what I've earned."

"Well, I don't suppose you're involved and don't think your help would do anything like that without orders. I'm left with only the ones who knew Borker was Interpol. That would be their own little group."

"Niko did tell me that someone said there is a man here from the world police. He heard about it at the ferry ... never mind. It is rumor."

They chatted a bit. Clint soon headed home. Maybe they could narrow it down to the one who actually killed him.

Or two?

Regardless, Clint wanted all of them out of Panamá. The one who killed an Interpol agent was going to be prosecuted all the way.

CD went down by the ferry dock where he saw Smith talking to Boko. He went to them and introduced himself. He said he was going to find the one who killed Borker.

"You for real, Man?" Smith said, with a sneer. "Ain't nobody here offed the turkey. It were one of his buddies, Man!"

"There was a wire around his neck?" Niko asked. "It wasn't us. We know fifty ways to eliminate people without using more than your hands and feet."

"I heard it was a wire and he got stuck," Smith said. "Getting stuck is an occupational hazard. No wire around the neck. Why both?"

"Why, indeed? So you could say you would never do it that way?" CD replied. "Do you know who he was?"

"He was just a fucking gringo tourist," Smith snarled. "Ain't enough of them getting offed!"

"Then you wouldn't have anyone to rip off. Think about it! Why are you here?" Clint fired back. "A ladron has to have somebody to steal *from*!"

"You got a mouth, Man! Maybe I'll off another one for kicks!"

"Give it a go, hotshit! You've got a body twice my size and a brain ten percent of my size!"

"Stop it! Both of you!" Niko demanded. "I'll kick both your asses!"

CD laughed. "You could probably do it."

"So you'd just shoot me. Hai, karate! Hai, forty five!"

"Do you know who offed him? Really?"

"I don't. Smith might."

"Nah. What you mean, 'Know who he was?' He was nobody!"

"He was Interpol, so they'll come here and tear this place apart if I can't find who killed him first."

"Shit!" Smith said.

"That's about my reaction. Mama Chiang is going to be very upset about this," Niko said. He took out a cell phone and called a number. He said he'd found that Borker was an Interpol agent, that there was going to be trouble. They had to be able to give them the one who killed Borker. He listened a minute, then rang off.

"Mama Chiang already knew it. I'll never know how she always knows everything about anything before anybody else."

CD knew Clint was going to talk to her. He could tell them ... nah!

CD went to find Anders, who had already talked with Clint the day before.

If it was one of this group it would be Boko.

He went to find Boko, who claimed to have been in Changuinola to collect some payments for Mama Chiang the time of the murder.

He would be alibied by someone, CD had no doubt. He thought he could believe it, despite that.

He headed for the house.

Nick stopped at the Grill to say hello. Jim was there, and David and Bob and Aaron.

And Tom, of course. Tom was saying he was going to write a book about this case. He had it figured out. Mama Chiang had him knocked over because he was the brains and was planning to open a little mall over close to the cemetery that would include a casino and bar and stores. He would compete with prices while no one there now ever did. It was about time he wrote another one.

"Oh? You write books? What kind?" CD asked

"Oh, whatever. Things like this come up. I can almost always figure them out, so I write about it."

"I know a man who writes books here. Dave. He's had more than a hundred fifty published."

"Er, um. Yes. I know him. He's used some of my ideas."

"Oh, come on! Dave thinks you're a total ass!" Bob snapped. "He's already shown you up! Why don't you have the sense to stop while you're ahead?

"CD, was it? Dave marched Tom and several of the rest of us to the internet café at Don Chicho's and looked up his book. It was a vanity press thing that didn't sell a hundred copies, total! Dave's got the first nine pages when you Google or Yahoo! search his name!

"Tom likes to dig a hole and fall into it."

"My book sold the entire first publishing!" Thom protested.

"It was POD! That's one book!" Bob shot back.

Tom got up and stomped off. Jim laughed and said, "Bob thinks about as much of Tom as Clint."

"Yes. I can see why, though something he said did help a lot. About the Chinese and the bunch arguing.

"You found out who Borker was yet?"

"I hear he was FBI, but that was from Tom, so it was nothing like that. We said maybe CIA, but he went into why the FBI is taking over the CIA. He heard it from a personal friend who's head of certain covert operations in the FBI."

"Oh? Tom knows a legal aide on apprenticeship at the FBI offices in Two Eggs, Florida?"

They laughed and said they didn't believe it was anyone that high on the scale.

After a few more minutes Nick went to the Sagitario Hotel to talk with Billings and Healey. They were staying at the cheapest hotel on Isla Colón while they opened a big project?

They didn't know who killed Borker. They had no idea why he was killed.

"He was working with Interpol. Did you know that?" Nick asked innocently. Healey dropped his beer. Billings looked like he'd been slapped with a rotted dead fish.

"I can see you didn't. Bad scene, huh?"

"Oh, God *damn*!" Billings cried. "I should have known Harry would bring in someone to fuck up the works. He's always been a fuck-up! Christ!"

"You've known him far a long time?"

"He came to Galveston about six years ago. He said he was working for a company that the FBI raided and he barely was able to show them he wasn't involved. It gave him the idea ... well, that's over now. I just want to get back home and never have to think about this mess again!"

"We're lucky, in a way. We haven't done anything illegal."

"Yet," Nick said. Healey nodded and looked grim.

"Except maybe kill him?" Nick added.

"If we'd known, the last thing we'd do would be bring the damned Interpol down on our heads! Christ!" Billings cried.

Nick could believe that. He eliminated these two. That left three.

He went back and saw Stoner and Stine sitting at The Pirate. He went in and said, "Hi! Just talking with Billings and Healey. They're getting out of here as fast as they can. They didn't know Borker was Interpol and don't want to be around when they come to investigate.

"I guess you'll want to go, too."

Stoner stared and looked like he'd faint. He was suddenly pale and sweating. Stine looked hard and grim.

"So. You killed Borker," Nick said to Stine. "You're the only one who knew Borker was Interpol."

"No. I didn't kill anybody and I'm not the only one who knew. One of our group knew and one Panamanian. I found out about it just before he was killed."

"There's only one more in your group. Kroner. There are things about Kroner that say he didn't kill anybody that way. He's not big enough, for one thing.

"So! Who's the Panamanian?"

Clint thought about it. It only added up one way. He sighed and decided to get it over.

CD carefully considered what he'd learned. He called Sergio and requested an address and told him why. Sergio would meet him there.

Nick went over what had happened and what he'd heard. It only added up one way. He knew where to go because he'd passed the place while he was walking the town.

Harley Anders saw Clint coming and sighed. He guessed he knew Clint would figure it out.

There comes that CD character. With Sergio? Did Clint really think he wold need help?

What the hell! Now that Nick person is coming around the corner! He wasn't holed up with an AK47! They didn't need a SWAT team!

Clint was coming onto the porch and saw Anders staring over his shoulder, so turned. Sergio and CD coming from directly across and Nick coming from the corner. He grinned at Anders. Anders said, "What the hell, Clint?"

"I guess we all figured it at the same time. We were working from the same information. You're the only one who didn't quite fit.

"Why did you kill him, Harley?"

"He was Interpol. He caught me carrying some pirate stuff to Almirante and stopped me there and said he was going to have me arrested and charged with international commerce in stolen jewels. I figured there was a fifty-fifty chance you would tag one of his buddies he didn't get along with for killing him."

"None of them had anything to do with it?" CD asked. Anders shrugged. "No."

"He was Interpol," Sergio said. "There's no way out."

"I know, " Anders replied. "Can I have tonight to straighten up all this shit around here?"

"If you promise not to run."

"Okay. What time tomorrow?"

"I come on duty at one, so be there then. Bring a toothbrush and all that crap."

"Okay."

"And that was it!" Nick exclaimed. Janet grinned.

"We're a lot more civilized here than in the states," Tyna said. "Clint usually just makes them leave Panamá. We don't need the expense of feeding and housing them for the next twenty years. This one is Panamanian, so we do have that."

"Borker was Interpol. Won't they send him to France or something?" CD asked.

"No. So far as Panamá is concerned, it was a murder to avoid exposure in Panamá and was committed by a Panamanian, so he gets tried and convicted here," Clint said. "The others in that little group will be sent on their sordid ways and declared undesirables, so they can't ever come back. The evidence, particularly against Stine, is already there, waiting for him. Kroner won't ever find decent employment in Germany again. The rest, I couldn't care less."

"Well, I'll head for David this morning. Alma will be waiting. I'd, personally, prefer to stay right here for the next fifty years or so, but I promised."

"You're welcome to stay as long as you like," Tyna said.

"We're going to stay here for the rest of our two weeks," Janet said, "I hope to be a regular visitor! This place is paradise!"

"You'll have to get used to our ways. Clint especially," Tyna warned. "Clint, go swimming and put on some clothes. We have visitors!"

Clint had forgotten to put on anything. He never did before he had his breakfast and a swim. Niko had come in and was just coming back from the beach. He and Nicole. They would get dressed and go to school.

"I'll run you to Chiriqui Grande, CD. It's no trouble. Really!" Clint said.

"I want to ride the cayuca. It also lets me stay here a little longer."

Clint and Nick went to the water and swam awhile. They waved when Nito, Nicole and CD headed for Cusapín, then when Janet and Tyna went the same way ten minutes later.

"I've never been a nudist before. This is great!" Nick said. Clint agreed. "We're not built any different than anyone else. I'm comfortable like this.

"Tyna left breakfast for us. Janet fits perfectly here. She's volunteered to help with the cacao this morning. My people feel we all have a duty to the community.

"I'm going to work with preparing a field for frijoles. You can laze around or whatever you like."

"I'll help with the frijoles. As good as these people are to me, I feel like one of you."

Clint nodded. They went to the house, dressed, ate the breakfast, and headed for town.

Nick Storie felt he was the luckiest man in the world!

Clint wondered what was coming next. He really did like a puzzle!

C. D. Moultons works are available on most major outlets as printed or e-books. CD writes the CD Grimes, Pi mysteries, the Det. Lt. Nick Storie mysteries, the Clint Faraday mysteries, the Flight of the Maita science fiction series, books on orchid culture and many others of many types. Mystery, adventure, intrigue, science fiction, fantasy, paranormal, mild erotica, and factual.